Mirror Story

Jez Alborough

LONDON • VICTOR GOLLANCZ LTD • 1988

The new gilt mirror, a present from Mr Featherby's mother, was hanging in the hall in Featherby House feeling very sorry for herself.

"What's wrong with me?" she asked her new friend, the wooden looking glass. "Why do Mr and Mrs Featherby always walk past me, yet invariably stop to look into you?"

"It's probably because you're new," suggested the looking glass. "Once they become accustomed to having you here, I'm sure they'll start looking into you, too."

"But what can I do until then?" sulked the new mirror. "All I have to reflect is this boring chair."

"There's nothing to do," replied the looking glass, "except be yourself; and remember — a true mirror always reflects faithfully whatever is in front of it."

Later that morning Mr Featherby walked past the new mirror but stopped to examine his profile in the looking glass. The new mirror was puzzled to note that Mr Featherby seemed unhappy with his reflection, until he had taken a deep breath and pulled in his stomach.

"He does that because he's getting fat," explained the looking glass, when Mr Featherby had left for work. "It makes him look thinner and then he feels happier with himself. Sometimes I think he would like me to bend the truth a little to make him appear slim, but that I'll never do. In my experience one deception always leads to another and, in the end, a single truth is less hurtful than a string of fibs."

The mirror didn't understand, but she noticed with interest that when Mrs Featherby walked by, she, too, was unhappy with her reflection in the looking glass. It was only after she had lifted her chin and sucked in her cheeks that she seemed satisfied with her appearance.

Seeing all this gave the mirror an idea.

"If I could find a way to make Mr and Mrs Featherby look slimmer, I'm sure they would begin to take notice of me," she thought. "Surely one little fib can't do much harm if it makes them happy, and besides — no one would know."

But how could she make them look thinner? The polished knob on the dining room door gave her the answer, for in it she noticed a squashed, wide reflection of herself.

"If, by being rounded and curved outwards, the door-knob can make me look fat, then surely by curving myself inwards, I can make Mr and Mrs Featherby look thin," she reasoned.

Carefully she twisted and shifted, straining her body until she had managed to pull herself in at the middle.

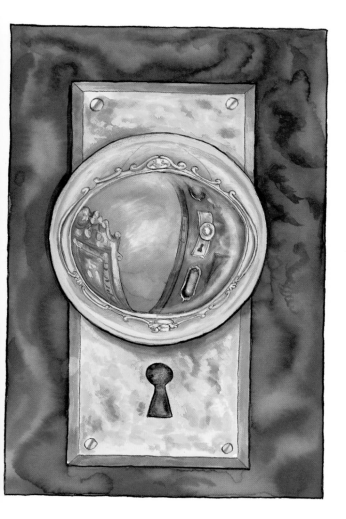

Later that summer afternoon, Mrs Featherby noticed her reflection as she passed the mirror. She could hardly believe her eyes. Looking back at her was the face of a younger woman whose cheeks were soft and shapely. Realising with delight that the face was her own, Mrs Featherby smiled, and the mirror, quite naturally, thought she was smiling at her.

When Mr Featherby returned that evening, he caught sight of his body in the new mirror. He grinned broadly, for there he saw not the usual portly girth but a trim, defined waistline.

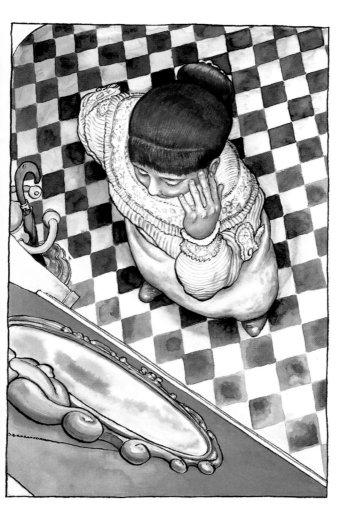

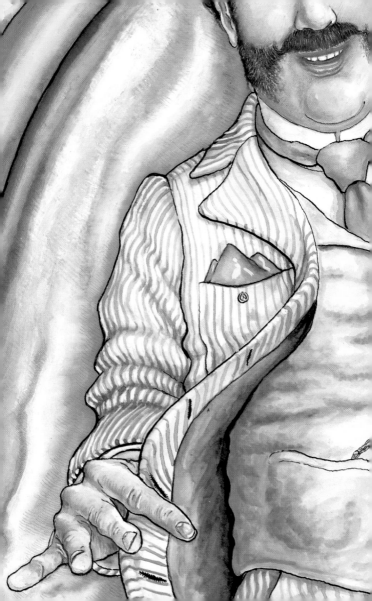

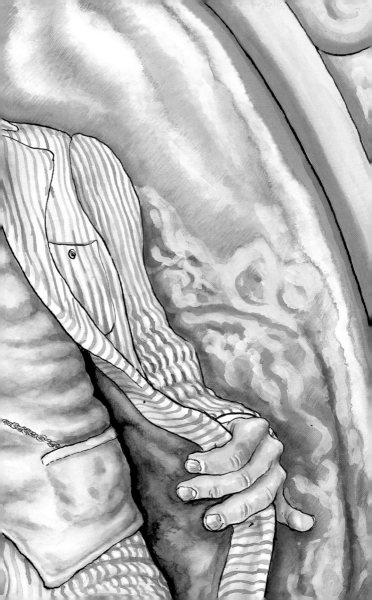

Unbeknown to each other, Mr and Mrs Featherby repeatedly crept back to the mirror throughout that evening, stealing sly peeps at themselves. The mirror felt enormously important — she was getting all the attention, and every time Mr and Mrs Featherby simpered at their reflections, she, of course, imagined that they were beaming at her.

"You're suddenly very popular," said the looking glass in surprise.

"Er . . . yes, you were right," stuttered the mirror hastily. "Now that they're used to me, I'm not ignored anymore."

"It would appear that our faithful looking glass has become too old to do its job properly," said Mr Featherby, at the dinner table, as he cut himself a second portion of ham. "Lately I have noticed that it has begun to distort."

"Quite right dear, I have noticed it too," agreed Mrs Featherby, as she helped herself to another boiled potato. "But we don't need it now that we have the lovely new mirror that your mother gave us."

Mr Featherby rose from the table. "I shall take the old thing down right away," he said, "and in the morning Ruby shall help me carry it up to the attic."

Hearing this alarming news through the dining room door, the mirror started to tremble on her hook.

"What have I done?" she cried, as Mr Featherby lifted the looking glass off the wall and on to the hall chair opposite her. "Now my new friend will spend the rest of his days gathering dust, with nothing to reflect but darkness — and it's all my fault!"

Suddenly she became aware of her own distorted image, thinly squeezed in the looking glass. She looked further into the reflection, on and on as if she were seeing into her very self; and the deeper she looked the more troubled and twisted she became.

"I have been unfaithful to the truth," she sobbed. "I've fibbed to Mr and Mrs Featherby, I've deceived my friend . . ."

"But most of all," interrupted the looking glass, "by pretending their smiles were for you, you've fooled yourself."

"But what will happen to you?" asked the mirror remorsefully. "Will they really banish you to the attic?"

"I can't tell what will happen," replied the looking glass calmly, "but I do know that the truth will come out in the end."

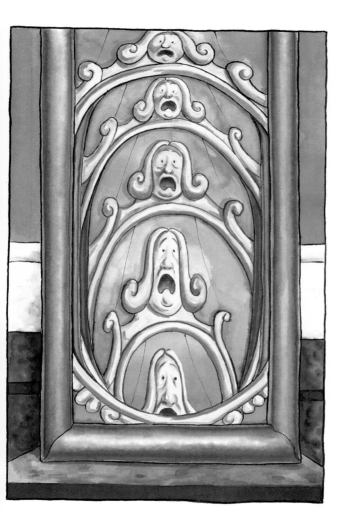

At the breakfast table the next morning, Mr Featherby announced, "I have a confession to make, my dear. I realised when I saw myself in the bathroom mirror last night that I've been deluding myself. I'm afraid I chose to believe the new mirror, rather than the old looking glass, because it flattered me by making me appear thin ... but the truth is, I'm not slim, I'm really rather portly."

"What a coincidence! When I saw my reflection in the dressing table mirror, it dawned on me that I have been less than honest too," admitted Mrs Featherby. "My face isn't as fine as the new mirror would have me believe; my cheeks are quite plump!"

"But you wouldn't be the same without your pretty, rounded face," said Mr Featherby affectionately.

Mrs Featherby blushed. "Why, thank you," she said. "And I'm fond of your portly tum. It makes you look distinguished."

Mr and Mrs Featherby smiled contentedly. Together they went out to the hall and lifted the looking glass back on to its hook.

"It's the new mirror that must go up to the attic," said Mr Featherby.

However, when they went to remove her and saw their reflections they were taken by surprise. There before them was a plump-cheeked lady and a distinguished-looking gentleman.

"Perhaps we imagined the whole thing," said Mr Featherby. "This is a true reflection and I like it. Mother's present must stay exactly where it is."

Mrs Featherby patted his paunch affectionately.

"What shall I do?" whispered the mirror. "I think they're going to kiss . . ."

The looking glass giggled. "That's simple," he said. "Just tell the truth."